PRAISE FOR THE HONEY MONTH

"...a great gift for lovers, especially lovers of the raw, the sweet, and the sticky."

ALEXANDRA ERIN
AUTHOR OF *TALES OF MAGICAL UNIVERSITY*

"Amal El-Mohtar exploded the speculative poetry world like a nova—and here she turns her dream-like attention to prose. Like nothing else you've read, *The Honey Month* is a strange and radiant hybrid of foody passion, sly sensuality, and geeky obsession of the best kind."

CATHERYNNE M. VALENTE
AUTHOR OF *PALIMPSEST*

"A word-posy for all the senses, a jar of golden windows into worlds: I savoured Amal El Mohtar's *The Honey Month* on a wooden honey dipper, stringing out her artful and chancy stories and poems over days in delicious slow loops of sweetness. The artist of me applauds her painterly skill: the colour of these words is amber-ochre. And I was smitten by the utter sensuousness of this wonderfully flavoursome book."

RIMA STAINES
ARTIST AND KEEPER OF *THE HERMITAGE*

"As you tuck into Amal El-Mohtar's *The Honey Month*, I would recommend having at the ready a big plate of warm crusty bread oozing butter and a few jars of honey with spoons at the ready. Yes, it will make you that hungry, that desirous of the sticky, glorious stuff. Honey is one of those mythical foods—celebrated in almost every culture for its potency, its golden sweetness as well as its amber bitterness. It is rubbed on the tongues of newborns to give them a good life, the faces of brides to make them fertile, and the hands of the dead to reward them in the afterlife. It is alchemy at its best—fragrant and edible.

So it is great fun to read Amal's salute to the glorious stuff in sensual, dreamy works of mythic poetry and short fiction. Scent and taste evoke emotions, memories, longings and each honey is introduced with its appropriate synesthesic qualities: Thistle honey has both "crispness and mellowness at once...playful, a child among honeys," while garnet red Blackberry Creamed Honey has the scent of "bread served at funerals." The literary responses to these sensory descriptions are steeped in the wax of fairy tale, romantic poetry, and memoir: a bee's stinger leads a dreamer to the lonely realm of a fallen star child; a wily lover seduces a young woman with proffered taste of peach cream honey; and a beloved childhood ring lost in the woods reappears a year later on the branches of a sapling."

MIDORI SNYDER
AUTHOR OF *THE INNAMORATI* AND CO-DIRECTOR, WITH TERRI WINDLING, OF THE ENDICOTT STUDIO FOR MYTHIC ARTS

THE HONEY MONTH

AMAL EL-MOHTAR

PAPAVERIA PRESS

www.papaveria.com

THE HONEY
MONTH

for Danielle Sucher & Cat Valente

INTRODUCTION

I met Amal in passing, a whirl of energy and glee at a small convention where Cat Valente was the guest of honor and I was catering the VIP suite. They say you know your best friends better within five minutes of meeting them than you know other people after twenty years of knowing each other, and maybe they're right, because we were off and running from the start. Next thing you know, I sent her thirty some odd vials of honey, little licks to sample and taste and write her impressions upon. I never dreamed what she could do with such meager inspiration. But remember, we'd only just met. I know better now.

She wrote her honey girls a day at a time during that February, the month Cat's novel *Palimpsest* came out. And every day I thought of the smell of beeswax and the buzzing that comes when you work with bees. I thought of the hives Roger keeps in the backyard of his church up in the Bronx, with smoke from leaves he saves each autumn to calm the ladies whenever he works with them, and the honey extractor down in the rectory basement. I thought of girls I'd known and been and wanted to meet and thought I could fall in love with, of stings I've felt and kisses I'd ached for.

She tracked my life with this project, perhaps more than she ever realized along the way. All of these honeys had lives before my pantry, overwritten by my finding and gathering of them, overwritten by their lives in tiny vials flown across the sea, overwritten again by Amal's impressions of them and the gorgeous worlds inside her that she shares with us.

About five years ago, I got it into my head that I wanted to keep bees. Beekeeping was illegal in NYC at the time, though, which posed a bit of a hurdle for me. I knew some folks did it anyway, but hadn't a clue how to find them. But life's not so complicated, and these things are doable. I called a friendly stranger out of the blue, met up with some urban agriculture organizations, and started hassling local politicians at parties. It gained momentum, as these things do—when I read about November's bees in *Palimpsest*, I thought they were the dream of mine.

My parents offered to let me keep a hive out in their house near Sag Harbor, by the bay. The bees could dine on beach plums and peach blossoms, and all the wild flowering things that grow up out of the silt. I declined on account of the commute, but the dream of it came back to me when I read Amal's vignette on the 3rd day of the honey month. How could she have known I almost kept bees by that harbor myself? I knew I would have to print these out and bring them to the beekeeper who now sells her honey in Sag Harbor, who always asks after my mother, who gives me tastes of honey on toothpicks, a lick at a time. Now, I look back on the thought of winter and anticipate dusting for Varroa mites by sprinkling powdered sugar over the hive, snow bees rising up into the air covered in a different kind of sweetness.

All I remember about my first bee sting is that I was with my grandmother on our way to the bus. The one near the good falafel place, I think, or a block that looked a lot like the falafel block from my little kid point of view. We were standing at the corner waiting for the light to change so we could cross, not far from a garbage can stinking in the summer heat. I don't remember the pain of it; I just remember crying endlessly as my grandmother scraped a butter knife across my skin to get the stinger out, and bathed the offending area in vinegar to end the pain.

I thought of that moment on the 23rd day, when the tart cherry girl walks away from the boy who smells of tobacco and molasses. Tobacco is an old folk remedy for bee stings, you see, to end the pain. Would he have ended her pain? Or did she do well to lose the courage to confront him? I don't know. I only know what it's like to be that girl, trying to rely on the strength of my want, and ultimately fearing to approach the boys who never saw me or wondered at my name.

The 15th day brought me back to Hungary, where my grandmother was born. She lost more than a ring to that country, stolen first by the Nazis and hounded out again by the Communists. She survived Auschwitz. She bargained her husband back from generals with sacks of grain and a baby on her hip, a young wife barely free from imprisonment and starvation herself. She fought her way out. But I have never seen her look so young and happy as when we went back to visit the little towns where she grew up, fifty years or so after she left.

Her old house was stolen when she fled the country. When we returned, it had become a post office. My frail old grandmother marched straight up to the postal worker behind the window and declared to her in furious Hungarian, "This is my house!" (I suspect I've bowdlerized her language a bit in paraphrasing from memory.) She never did lack for courage. And she never did get her house back.

Our stories are so similar and so intertwined, Amal's and mine. My family's home was stolen from them, in a nightmare that has echoed through our lives down the generations; Amal's loved ones have had their homes and lives stolen as well, in a story too similar for comfort. There is a damaged palimpsest between us, rewritten again and again until nothing is legible and nothing is right. As Amal put it, our people's palms are too full of thorns to hold hands, even though they match.

The Honey Month isn't about that conflict, and I don't want to get too sidetracked by it here. But I want you to understand this: every honey has its story, and if some of those stories are darker and more complicated than we might like, so be it. The 11th day tells both our stories. Our only choice is where to take them next.

As for me, after five years of wanting, waiting, and fighting for legalization, I'm finally setting up my first hive this spring. Forty thousand fuzzy little pets to love and call my own and suffer for with sticky sweetness and poison and death, alarm pheromones that smell like angry bananas, and one stately slave queen doing her work at the bidding and tolerance of the rest.

I reread all the poems and stories that follow before sitting down to write this introduction, and found for the first time after reading them together that Amal had presented my life back to me as reflected by her own strange facets. I hadn't realized that day by day she was rewriting me without either of us noticing what was happening there. And now that she has, I can't help but think that there is no one I'd trust more to do it.

It is an honor to reach out and hold her hand.

∾ *Danielle Sucher*

Day 1 ~ Fireweed honey

Smell: Slightly resinous, warm, not very strong.

Colour: Mellow gold, an almost "typical" honey colour—what you'd imagine saying "honey tones" would mean, referring to hair or wood.

Taste: Gentle. Very similar to clover honey, but not quite as sweet: mellow, kind. No unusual notes; all I can think is "mm, honey," but without that extra quality that makes me so keenly understand the line from *Romeo and Juliet* where honey is "loathsome in its own deliciousness," where the sweetness takes on an added dimension so different from sugar, in a way that scrunches your nose when you're a child but closes your eyes when you're grown up. If I were to attempt to be sophisticated I'd say it was understated. Delicious, all the same.

Come to me, she said, *and I will plait fireweed into your hair. When you laugh, it will gleam like wheat in sunlight, and when you weep, it will sweeten your tears until hummingbirds are drawn to sip them. Only come to me, and be my love, for I am so alone, and there is no one to tend the hives with me, no one to tip the moon-water from my well, no one to hold my hand in the dark. The night is cold and the moon is colder, and my sisters have all forgotten me.*

So spoke the star-girl, many years fallen, when I dreamed of her that night.

I had gone to bed with my left arm throbbing. I was rooting around in the spice cupboard when I cried out, yanked my hand back in surprise; a bee had been wintering there, had stung me just above the wrist, and now wriggled in her death throes between jars of honey and cinnamon. I had never been stung before, and marvelled at how much it hurt.

It seemed cruel to let her suffer, but I couldn't bring myself to mangle her any further. I scooped her up, dropped her out on the windowsill, and went to find some garlic to rub on the sting.

I thought the dream was the garlic's fault, at first.

There was a mountain in the distance, and a glowing at its foot. I walked towards it, as one does in dreams, and found I could smell heat, a smell like warm water and beeswax candles, that grew stronger the closer I got. Soon I began to see strange bushes all around, a gold-green spread along the mountain's edge, full of rust-red flowers that glowed against the darkness.

It took me a moment to notice the girl by the well. She did not smile at me. She didn't look as if she could.

Her skin was pale as quartz, clear and clouded in the same way; her eyes were like water, and shone painfully. She had no hair, no eyebrows, but her face was perfect, cabochon-smooth, and she was crying.

It is pointless to say she was beautiful. It cannot mean what I want it to mean. When I looked at her I wanted both to touch her and watch her from a distance, to hold her and hide from her, to kiss her and ask her to forgive me—for what, I couldn't say, except that she looked so sad.

She did it, she said. Tears shone against her cheeks. *She found someone. Stay longer, next time, please?*

Before I could answer her, I woke up.

It was still dark out. I got out of bed, made myself some tea. I couldn't say what it was about the star-lady that had shaken me. It was so hard to remember dreams, usually, but this one followed me from home to work and back again. I crawled into bed early, wanting the dream back, but didn't hope for it too strongly. On the rare occasions I'd dreamed something beautiful—the beginning of an adventure, the opening of a novel beckoning me on to the next chapter—it was impossible, no matter how much I willed it, to pick up the thread I'd dropped.

I had no trouble this time.

You came back, she said, and I melted to see her almost smile, to see hope kindle in her adamantine eyes. *She thorned you deep. Will you stay?*

I tried to ask her name, who she was, but the dream-speech tangled in my mouth, threatened to wake me if I forced it. She understood.

I fell. We must guard against the slightest fall, against even the thought of it; a fall is never slight to us. Something in us is always wanting the plunge, the speed, the disgrace, and once we taste weightlessness we become gluttons for it.

I was very beautiful, then, with my eight-pointed hair bound up in fireweed. My sisters called me their little opal, though they were all so much lovelier than me. I was playing a chase-game with them when I tripped against this mountain's tip, back when mountains still grew and sought to tickle us in our beds. I tripped, and the falling had me, and all my eight-pointed hair burned behind me, and my fireweed too, except for one bit, one tiny bit I kept clutched in my fist for all that it hurt so sharp.

I planted it. I watered it with kisses and tears and moon-slicked water from this well, and it grew to heat and brightness again. I tried to climb up the mountain, but by the time I was halfway up it had forgotten how to grow, gone drowsy, began to decline. All things seek to fall, in time. It is not nearly tall enough for me now, and I am trapped, and alone, save for my fireweed, my bees, and this well. The bees love the moon-water; it is sweeter than sugar. Will you help me feed them?

How could I not?

I never thought to ask, then, how I could stay with her when I was bound to wake up. I never thought to wonder how I would rearrange my life to live less and sleep more, that I might draw her moon-water and feed her bees, that I might kiss her cool cheeks and tell her stories. I never thought, and I should have, because here I am, still, and I wonder if I can wake up now, wonder if I am laid out in my bed with someone knocking at the door I can't answer, wonder if it will take someone to suck the sting from my wrist before I can leave.

I don't know. It's always night, here, and she is always so beautiful. The hummingbirds, too. They never seem to leave.

Day 2 ~ Peach Creamed Honey

Colour: Pale and cloudy, like lemonade.

Smell: Rather unpleasant; sweaty underthings, but with a hint of lemon beyond it.

Taste: Oh, so delicious. Sweet, syrup-sweet, thick and sugary. I have to think of peaches to discern a peachy flavour; it comes out at the back of my mouth, the top of my throat. It's a mischievous honey, sexy and wry.

They say
she likes to suck peaches. Not eat them, suck them,
tilt her head back and let the juice drip
sticky down her chin, before licking, sucking,
swallowing the sunshine of it down. They say
she likes to tease her fruit, bite ripe summer flesh
just to get that drip going
down, down,
sweets her elbow with the slip of it,
wears it like perfume.

I say
she's got a ways to go yet, that girl,
just a blossom yet herself, still bashful 'round the bees. I say
no way a girl can tease like that
who's been bit into once or twice.

So I come 'round with just a little bit of honey,
just a little, little lick, just enough to catch her eye,
creamed peach honey, just the thing to bring her by.
And I know she'll let me tell her how the peaches lost their way
how they fell out of a wagon on a sweaty summer's day,

how the buzz got all around that there was sugar to be had,
and the bees came singing, and the bees came glad.
They sucked—she'll blush—I'll tell her, they sucked that fruit
right dry,
'till it all got tangled up in the heady humming hive.
They made it into honey and they fed it to their queen,
and she shivered with the sweet, and she licked the platter clean,
and she dreamed of sunny meadows and she dreamed of soft ice
cream—

I'll see her lick her lips, and I'll see her bite a frown,
and I'll see how she'll hesitate, look from me up to the town
and back, and she'll swallow, and she'll say "can I try?"
and I'll offer like a gentleman, won't even hold her eye.

Because she'll have to close them, see. She'll have to moan a bit.
and it's when she isn't looking
when she's sighing fit to cry,
that I'll lick the loving from her,
that I'll taste the peaches on her
that I'll drink the honey from her
suck the sweet of her surprise.

Day 3 ~ Sag Harbor, NY, Early Spring Honey

Colour: Pale and clear as snowmelt, just about as much colour as a Riesling.

Smell: The colour must be affecting me—but, crystals, cool sugar crystals. If honey were water. As I pull it out of the imp, I think of a stingless jellyfish I once held in the palm of my hand, in Oman. Very faint hint of citrus, too, but more grapefruit than lemon.

Taste: This honey tastes like winter. No—it tastes like the end of winter, but not quite spring. It tastes like those days where you can still see clumps of snow on the ground and the air is heavy with damp but it all smells so *good* because snowmelt is like that, the trees are black and fragrant though they've barely begun to bud. Refreshing; the sweetness isn't cloying, it's faint and gentle and almost an afterthought. My favourite so far.

Not every harbour has a hive, but those that do are wise enough to know themselves blessed.

It cannot be too salty a harbour; it must be at the widening mouth of a river trying to swallow the sea. It must drink the rising, not the setting, sun. It must bear boats safely into it, look calmly into the eyes of a storm and tell it that while it may bluster the trees, it may not ruffle the waters. Suppose it should spoil the honey and make it taste of *sturm und drang*?

The gathering happens in the spring, of course, the early spring. That is the time for coaxing sweetness from the world: sap from trees, scent from flowers. It needs to be tapped, needs to be gently drawn from its winter bed like a child on a chilly morning, sand in the lashes, dreams in the eye. It does not yet know itself to be sweetness; it is a snowdrop, not a rose.

So it happens in the early spring that the harbour bees skim the water, and wait. The water is cold; it does not happen quickly. But eventually, oh! So slowly, the surface stretches like a skin, parts along the silky hair of a harbour-maid. Her eyes are the colour of dawn on the water, her mouth is a single lily, its five pale petals stretching along her cheeks, her chin, tickle her nose. The bee exults, carefully gathers what the girl will give while keeping its wings free of the water, and dances the news to the hive.

Slowly, slowly, other heads rise, other flower-mouthed girls with hair like snow, and the bees travel from one to the next, sipping the river nectar and weaving it into their hive. The girls smile with their eyes, thank the bees for their service—and when the bees have wriggled their gifts from each to each, the girls will sink back down into the water, close up the petals of their mouths, and dream of the bud-lipped children they will bear come fall.

DAY 4 ~ RASPBERRY ROSE HONEY

Colour: If yesterday was a Riesling, today is a Sauvignon Blanc. It's just-turned-dawn coloured, pale and clear with less yellow than a hint of gold to come. The consistency is also much thinner than any of the previous honeys; this is much more liquid, not a hint of cloud to it.

Smell: Very nearly odourless, but my first impression was of heat, of a roasted sweet, but then on second thought, no. Very faint hint of the unpleasant thick scent of the peach creamed honey, but that yielded such deliciousness, I'm delighted.

Taste: There's a hint of apple to this, but the rose! I taste rose petals, I taste *scent*. The raspberries are hidden— there's a faint bit of tartness to the aftertaste, and that's where they come out, but in the main it's golden apple-light and pink roses gilding themselves in dawn. This is so beautiful, subtle and balanced and entwined with itself.

Sleep now, my love, hush; I will lay this rose against your lips and you will breathe it in like a lullaby, let it lead you into sleep. Hush, my beauty, hush, my lovely, I will hang raspberries from your ears to draw the good dreams in, I will place honey on your tongue to sweeten your words to the princess you will meet among them, who will come riding a white cat with a silver buckle 'round its neck, who will bear a standard and a sword and a pen about her person, who will ask you to fight for her glory and her crown. She will call herself Queen of Roses, and you will see the garland that thorns her brow, and it will seem splendid and terrible and worthy of your strength. She will ask you to speak a poem to her, and when she does, you must say,

O Rose, aren't you sick
of metaphors, of perfection,
of being Queen to a grasping multitude
who've never brushed a thorn? Rose, I am sick
of these shadows you cast on pages, of cheeks
that would not know your colour
if it sweetened their pale lips.
Rose, I won't touch you,
I won't kneel to drink you in,
I won't write you odes or sonnets,
nor paint your gardens red. Rose,
only love me,
only let me speak this to you,
only judge me worthy of you,
and I will be content.

And when you have done this, her mouth will grow stern. She will frown at you, say you have displeased her, and to remedy this you must journey far afield to the fountain of topaz and rubies that lies in the land of Nod-on-Thorn, and once there you must drink from the fountain and fall into a thousand years' sleep, upon which time, if she has forgotten her displeasure, she will come with a lick of honey on her lips, press them against yours, and draw you back to wakefulness like water from a well.

DAY 5 ~ CRANBERRY CREAMED HONEY

Colour: Dark amber, cognac. Funny to me how I have such boozy associations, but they are apt.

Smell: There's a sharpness, a resinousness to this. It's also very liquidy.

Taste: A definite cranberry tartness, but the honey taste dominates; the tartness limns it, darts around its edges, makes it one of the more refreshing honeys I've tried. I think of pine, strangely, redwood; tasting it is like walking a forest path.

There is fire in his wrists, fire in his sharp-shod walk, fire beneath his fingernails. He is red, redder than rowan berries, for rowan doesn't bleed as cranberries do, and it is cranberries that he gathers, that he stews and crushes, cranberries in which he steeps his skin. Lacking a Mithrasian bull, he takes them, bathes in them, rinses his hair red-black, seeking transcendence.

It is not white, he says, *that is pure. It is not black. It is red, because it moves, it changes, and it keeps itself always. It is not static as fossilized wood, not delicate as new-fallen snow. When red seeks to be its truest self, it is in motion. It fears no change.*

He has shrugged at Paracelsus, at Tarot cards, at accusations of devilry. Red is his religion. He squeezes berry juice onto his eyelids, swallows it nine times a day, thrice at each meal. He wants the redness to spill from him like a scent, that in walking the forest paths the sleeping deer and wolves and rabbits will come to dream in garnet tones, will tremble and flush at the thought of pursuit, the game of the chase.

The bees dream red when he passes.

When they wake, their queen begins to wail. She needs it, she says, that red of reds that walks the woods like a shadow. The bees are dutiful, and go.

They find him, but do not know how to scrape the redness from him, cannot brush it against their bodies, cannot gather it like pollen. In vain they stamp his cranberry cheeks, in vain they buzz his cranberry ears. They cannot take a piece of him back to the hive.

Meantime he is beset by a phalanx of black-ribbed gold, drowns in the drone of their discontent. He swats at them, rages at them, gathers stings against the back of his hand, the curve of his elbow. What are these that come to gild his redness, limn his red thoughts with their bright noise? What are these that dare change his red shadow's shape, settling and rising like clouds at sea?

They madden him. They do not mean to. They hardly know that they are pushing him, driving him, herding the redness of him homeward.

Enough, says the queen, while he weeps in great red sobs. *Enough, that is enough.* She does not need to leave her childbed to imbibe him, only needs him to stay in the comb of her children's bodies, stay and share his colour with her. He cannot but comply.

She dreams, and her workers pour red into their gold, raise larvae with rust-red bodies, make honey heady as the setting sun. They weave it into their songs and dance its colour into the air they breathe. There is an orange to them, an amber, now – never quite red, for it is not the cranberry they love, but the shaping of their gold, the change, the sharpened edges to their queen's dreams.

He is in all they do, their most precious drone; they love him like a fine day. They look after him in their fashion. The bees go out, burrow into their sisters' bodies, sing their gladdest thanks against his lips. They go bearing their darkest honey, the densest, the best, the closest to the red they can never quite achieve, the redness that is his, only his. One by one, they place a drop on his tongue like a sacrament.

It is never red enough.

Day 6 ~ Lemon Creamed Honey

Colour: Pale yellow and cloudy, just about the colour of lemon flesh.

Smell: I've described others as having a faint citrus after-scent, but this one has a real lemon bite to it, makes me expect to see bits of pulp in the vial.

Taste: Refreshing. The lemon in this is like morning light, its sweetness juicy rather than sugary, without the slightest hint of tartness or sourness, like lemon and honey bind in a way that cancels out the less desirable qualities of each and marries only their virtues together. Delicious.

The lemon road is long, the lemon road is wide,
the lemon road is pleasant as a maid-sung song;
the lemon road will have you for its bride.

When first I turned my feet from the salt-stitched tide,
They told me I was foolish, told me I was wrong.
"The lemon road is long, the lemon road is wide,

it will sour all your footsteps, sour you inside.
Stay here with the brine, with us, where you belong—
the lemon road will have you for its bride."

I laughed at their warnings, but I couldn't—though I tried—
put them from my thoughts while I walked myself along.
The lemon road is long, the lemon road is wide,

and I felt myself pucker, felt a tightness in my side,
a frown on my lips, with the whisper growing strong:
the lemon road will have you for its bride.

My fingers all are yellowed, I struggle with my stride,
I hear a yellow laughter from a yellow-sounding throng.
The lemon road is long, the lemon road is wide—
the lemon road has got for me for its bride.

Day 7 ~ Thistle honey

Colour: Sauvignon Blanc again; pale clear gold.

Smell: Similar to clover honey, light, with a tiny bit of green apple.

Taste: Intriguing—definitely an apple taste, definitely *green* apple, and again, this is one of the refreshing ones; there's a crispness and a mellowness at once, and I feel it's playful, a child among honeys, but a wise-eyed child, somehow, the kind to whom you'd speak seriously one moment before tickling the next.

The day I met Scraggle I was walking in the hills on a windy day, wearing a button-down blue cardigan half open over a yellow blouse.

"You look like summer," she said to me, and smiled. I smiled back. She was cute, sitting on a large grey rock; she looked about seven years old, with a wide mouth and round cheeks, tight button nose, blue eyes and curly brown hair. "Curly" is perhaps too generous; she was named for her hair, she'd later tell me, and it was a twig-tangled mess that day.

"You look a bit like summer yourself," I said, and she did, wearing a purple tank-top and tatty jeans in Cornish February. "Aren't you cold? Here," I shrugged out of my cardigan, held it out to her. "Put this on. Someone nick your jacket?"

She stared at me, looked from me to the cardigan, and I wondered what I'd done wrong, because I could've sworn she looked about to cry. Then she took the cardigan, bounced behind her rock, and disappeared.

There's no other way to say it. She was there, then she wasn't. I shivered all the way home.

It's strange, how your mind works in those situations. You spend years longing for your dreams to last longer, be more tangible, leave some piece of themselves in your waking world, but when something does happen, when you're confronted with the strange, suddenly it's a matter of finding any explanation but the obvious for what happened. I had none; my mind was still rational, if stunned. If I'd been hallucinating the whole thing, I'd probably have been a lot warmer.

Besides, she was sitting on my bed when I got home, cardigan and all. She looked at me warily.

"I only eat thistle honey," she said, defensively, "and it must be very fine. You may heat the juice of apples for me, too, and perhaps a bowl of milk and a new loaf of bread, but nothing else."

When I did nothing but stare at her—not my finest conversational moment, to be sure—she frowned. "You must know the terms of the compact. You snared me by them, after all. And all for being polite! Mother did warn me not to be polite," she muttered.

"You—how did you get in? You need three different keys—"

She rolled her blue eyes. "You are very stupid, summer-girl. I am hungry; I require honey before we come to any terms."

"But I don't have any—I mean, I've got, you know, regular honey, but—"

Her chin trembled, her eyes misted, and she started crying.

"You are *horrible*, summer-girl! Why would you do that? Why would you give me a skin just to see me starve? Mother will miss me and she will have to steal some ugly farmer's brat to replace me and they will soil my beds of sweet-peas and trample my asters and all because *you* wanted a thiskie all to yourself!"

"But I *don't!*" I wanted to give her a hug, but she was hugging herself tightly in that way that says *don't touch me, don't come near*, so I stayed put. "Honest—I have no idea what you're talking about. I don't even know your name—"

"Scraggle," she sniffed, rubbing her fingers into her eyes. "For my hair. You'll have to give me a new one."

"...Why?"

"Because I am *yours*, now, stupid, and you must name me and feed me and keep me for I may not name nor feed nor keep myself while I wear a skin of your giving! Don't you know *anything*?"

"But I didn't—oh!" I brightened. "You mean, the cardigan? I just didn't want you to be cold! You can give it back."

She tossed her head back in exasperation. "If you mislike your skin, can you give it back to your maker and request a new one?"

I suspected she probably wouldn't like an answer that involved cosmetic surgery, so I bit my lip. "So—you can't—I mean, there's no way to change this? I'm sorry, Scraggle—I just didn't know."

She sighed. "It's all right, I suppose. You do not seem cruel, for all that you are very stupid. You have freely given me a skin off your back, and I am at your service. Only find me some honey? Thistle honey, remember."

I frowned, thinking. "Is that why it happened? Because I gave it freely?"

She shrugged. "Of course. But I cannot buy it from you now; there is nothing that can repay the gift freely given except a life of service."

"But—" and I hoped very hard, "I didn't give it freely."

She squinted at me. "I was there, summer-girl. You asked for nothing in return."

"No, see—" and I grinned at her, "I gave it to you in *thanks*, see? For your compliment. Because you said I looked like summer, and that made me feel very beautiful, and I was in your debt, so I gave you the cardigan to repay—"

She vanished. The cardigan went with her.

I wished she'd have let me finish the sentence, let me see her relieved and happy again. But I figured the brush with magic was reward enough—not to mention escaping the expense of thistle honey on a grad student's budget.

I didn't go walking in the hills for a couple of weeks. I didn't want to, knowing I'd always be keeping an eye out for her and her rock, knowing I was setting myself up for disappointment. But one day I wandered into one of those organic cafes, the kind with the cloth-covered jams and ribbon-bound jars of cardamom jelly, and I saw a little glass container of thistle honey. I took a breath, decided I had enough tea and toast to last me a couple of days, and bought it.

The next day it rained, but I couldn't wait any longer. I stomped out onto the hills in wellies and a black slicker, jar of honey clutched tightly in hand. Hoping against hope that no one else would be in earshot, I yelled "Scraggle! *Scraggle!*"

"What, what? Ugh, I forget that summer is loud as bees. What is it, summer-girl?"

"I—" was overcome with delight, honestly. There she was, still wearing the cardigan—getting it soaked, mind, but still. "I—just brought you some—" at the warning look she gave me, I swallowed. "Listen, I was wondering if you would swap me that cardigan for this honey. Is that a fair trade?"

She pursed her lips, considering. "Is it thistle?"

"Of course," I said, trying to sound solemn.

"Done!" She clapped her hands, shrugged the cardigan off. "This is good. I was tiring of the colour."

I handed her the honey a little tensely, expecting her to vanish any second. I didn't dare say what I was thinking: that it made me happy to see her again, that I wished we could be friends, that I wanted to run down hills with her and ask her about her family. I didn't dare, because suppose there were rules? I couldn't afford a jar of overpriced specialty honey every time I wanted a glimpse of her, after all. So I kept quiet while she opened the jar, dipped her middle finger in, sucked, and closed her eyes happily.

"Well!" she said, screwing the lid shut, and vanishing the jar into a pocket of her tatty jeans. "Shall we go?"

"Go?"

She patted my knee, grinning. "Stupid summer-girl. Perhaps you'll be brighter when the rain's gone, just like the sun in summer! Yes, go. We can't have an adventure standing still."

The things you learn on soggy Cornish hills. Of course we couldn't. Nor did we. Who'd want to stand still in the rain?

DAY 8 ~ RASPBERRY CREAMED HONEY

Colour: Close to cognac but a little lighter, with a hint of pale pink rose when the light shines through it; also, very evenly cloudy.

Smell: Hmm. Similarly to the peach creamed honey, there's an unpleasantness—an odd non-food smell, like sugared belly-button fuzz, and warm.

Taste: *Pure raspberries.* Raspberries made golden. Tart sharpness made smooth, and it's amazing. Much clearer fruit taste than the other creamed honeys so far.

My feet were in the river when the dawn forgot to rise.

I saw it begin. I saw the light yawn against the water, saw it raise a rosy finger out to hook a cloud—and then saw it pull back, recede, vanish. I curled my toes into the silt. This was not how it was supposed to happen.

Stand barefoot in the water at dawn tomorrow and you shall receive a great gift, said the note. I had assumed it was my aunt, playing games; I thought she would be here standing next to me, back from her travels through Prague, Paris, Beirut, squeezing my shoulder and offering me raspberries. I thought that we would watch the dawn together. It was the sort of thing she would do.

But the dawn was gone, sucked back into the horizon, and I felt like I should know what to do.

As is sensible in such situations, I spoke to the river.

"Where, if you'll pardon my asking," I cleared my throat slightly, "is the dawn?"

"Being swallowed by the ogress," murmured the river. "She's pulled it from me like a tablecloth, and I am bare and cold when I should be warm."

"Why now? The dawn has risen for every day of the ogress' long life; why should she fancy a taste for it now?"

"Why not?" Shrugged the river. "She is an ogress; you'll find they're always hungry. Perhaps she ran out of raspberry creamed honey and thought the dawn an appropriate substitute."

I thought about this, and it seemed a good enough reason. "Does she hunger in her sleep?"

"Naturally," sighed the river, "but it's the dream-thief she troubles then, less so the dawn. I've no doubt it's he who woke her, to give himself some respite—but he brought it on himself, poor lad, and we can hardly give up the dawn... I would speak to her, but I am so cold, and she chews so loudly."

"Listen," I said, "I have an idea."

And I knelt down in the water, cupped the river to my lips. "My mother used to sing this to me," I said, "and it always put me to sleep. Tell it to the ogress, let her hear it, and perhaps it will do as well for her."

Now to sleep, now to sleep,
I'll pluck the flight of doves for you, I'll gather wool from sheep,
see, little dove, oh! would you believe,
how I murmur to the ogress in her sleep?

I sang verse after verse, and as the river never told me to stop, only dutifully repeated after me, I sang it all through. Songs whispered through rivers have a strange charm, after all, a strange and lilting sorrow from the wave. Slowly, as I neared the end of the song, I saw the sky begin to lighten; I sang it a second time, a third, and soon dawn was spilling out over the river like wine.

"Well," said my aunt from behind me, "I told you to stand, not kneel, but I suppose it's all one. What are you doing, all wet?"

I scrambled to my feet, turned around, sheepishly. "Where have you been? I waited, and then—"

"I said at dawn, didn't I? And here I am, and dawn's just woken, hasn't it?"

"But—"

"Here," she smiled. "I didn't bring you any raspberries this time, per se, but I found something better: raspberry creamed honey! The most charming young gentleman sold it to me in Prague for a song. He told me it would taste better than a stolen dream. Here, have a lick."

She was right. It did.

Day 9 ~ Zambian Honey

Colour: Mulled cider; caramelised orange peels.

Smell: Dry and fresh at once, like a windy wheat field. Sunshine—my first impression. Spring sunshine, golden without heat, because the wind's stolen it away. But also earth; not damp, but not cracked dry. Earth just shy of being dust, caked gold.

Taste: This is the first of the honeys to have crystallised in the vial; I drew the wand out covered in chunks. Oh, and it is dry and burnished, caramel tones, burnt-sugar tasting and thick, strong; close to buckwheat honey, that distinctive taste, brown. Makes me think of the scent of beeswax, and the darker colours of it, too.

I am cracked dry as the shell of a nut
I am baked brown as skin.
I am the earth, and you and I are kin.

You do not know me, little one
with your wings thin as sky
buzzing like rain. Do not fear me, do not
shy from my heat; see
how I push and strain to grow the sweet
from which you would be fed?
I would sweat
to show you my hard work
but I have no water in me,
no tears, no spit,
and my copper heart is broken,
all my beauties stolen
away.

Do not fly so far, my sweet,
my desert-striped musician;
I would know your little feet
against my cheek, my breast,
beaten hard into a deaf drum
without bone. No one
comes near, their sandals bruise me
my heat is too greedy, too grasping,
it burns as it longs.
But I would not burn you; your wings
would nuzzle the air against my brow
and I would know relief.

No? You shun me so?
Scorn me for my frankincense, my bare trees, their thorns?
I understand. They are not enough
to draw the delicate, the sippers of air,
the makers of sweetness and light. I see
that I am too rough, too brown
for your gold bands and your black.
Only the sun will touch me.

DAY 10 ~ FRENCH RHODODENDRON HONEY

Colour: The colour of sugar dissolving in hot water; that white cloudiness, with a faint yellow tint I can only see when looking at it slantwise, to the left of me, not when I hold it up to the light.

Smell: Strange, it has almost no scent at all; it's also crystallised, so it's a bit difficult to scoop some out with the wand, but it smells cold with an elusive citrus squirt hovering about its edges.

Taste: There is a kind of sugar cube my grandfather used to give my sister and me every morning when we were small, not so much a cube as a cabochon, irregularly rounded, clear and cloudy by turns. It was called *sikkar nabet*, which is "plant sugar." This tastes like it. The honey taste is so pale, so faint, it really is almost sugar water. I'm reminded of maple sap in buckets, right at the beginning of the boiling process that produces maple syrup, where it's still water enough to be used for steeping tea.

harbour in Penryn
the moon is a sugar-stone
melting on my tongue

quai bas à minuit:
la pleine lune fond contre ma langue
comme une jeune Française.

DAY 11 ~ BLACKBERRY HONEY

Colour: Dark amber, almost identical to a Betty Stogs bitter, ascertained by the fact that I held my imp up to a glass of the latter. Let it not be said that I am less than rigorous in my booze-inspired descriptions.

Smell: Faint and mellow; grass and earth, but not cut grass, not that mown-lawn smell, but a scent that's clean and warm and sweet. Caramel 'round its edges.

Taste: This tastes like a mouthful of ripe blueberries. Not so much black; there isn't that tart juiciness of the blackberry. It's much more the fleshy freshness of blueberries. That texture, in fact.

⚜

My body is a knot of limbs
and I dream of Alexander
of a clean bright blade to slice
through the tangle of what is left.

They pulled me from the rubble
like a fabled sword; never
was Excalibur so tarnished, never
did dustier hands reach
for so shattered a hilt.

Blueberries washed the ash from my tongue
after they came; after the metal and the phosphor
that washed us all so red, so white. Perhaps
if we powdered our cheeks so every day
they would come to think us beautiful?

We might ornament their lawns, their homes
that once were ours, their swimming pools
and tourist traps, their cafes and museums.
Behold! The savage Philistine
undone by David's sling! See
how his mighty giant's body
is limned in our pale chalk!
The Americans would love it,
buy a t-shirt to take home.

Yesterday I had daughters. Today
I have these berries on my tongue.

I am lucky, they say, to live; to have
blueberries and water, medicine for my wounds.
I am lucky, they say, to breathe
the air thick with stone
that was my house; safe in my lungs
who would think to take it?

I am lucky, they say, to sleep. To dream.
To lay my head where the Son of Man once did
and close my eyes. To think,
tomorrow I may yet wake
to better.

I cannot sleep.
The earth is knotted with screams.
I taste blueberries on my tongue
and dream of nothing.

DAY 12 ~ RED GUM HONEY

Colour: Another in the white wine series. This one has much of dawn over rivers to it, says Italian Pinot Grigio to me.

Smell: Pie crusts just shy of brown. A hint of molasses.

Taste: A perfect honey. It's all gold brown and dark sugar, all mellow, its texture that languorous liquid that makes women sing *slow like honey* in aching voices. It has this beautiful elasticity to it; I can twirl it around the imp's wand like I'm using it to sign my name. There's a vanilla flavour here, that must be the baking association. But it also casts my mind back to the first honeys I tasted, and I can't remember at all, now, when I first tasted honey—I think it must have been in a pita wrap with cheese, that's how my mother would have served it. I'll have to ask her. Meantime it's childhood and my grandmother and the word *aassal*, and while I'm acutely aware of the *each lovelier than the last* dynamic in most of these descriptions, I think this is my favourite one to date.

She drinks the light like lemonade,
sips it bit by liquid bit,
until the day falls dark and soft
licked slow-as-honey clean.

Her throat is wide as an open door
inviting, honest, full of song,
and the light, it wants it, tumbles in
like a girl after a rabbit.

She swallows every now and then
licks her lips, parts them for more.
Every now and then, she sleeps.

While she does, the Moonish man
builds his nets, chases his dog.

She would take him by the hand
look into his eyes, and say,
love, you should know better now.

The world is not for catching, love
not for having, not for keeping.
The world is all for sipping, love
so tilt back your head and drink.

But he will never hear her, so
preoccupied with precious plans.
He has no willing ear to lend,
while he mutters on and on.

She wakes to quiet loneliness,
dresses, walks to her windowsill,
and sip by sip, lick by lick,
draws night back home again.

Day 13 ~ Black Locust Blossom Honey

Colour: Wine-gold dawn.

Smell: White flowers tucked into honeycomb. A watery white flower—lotus, or lily.

Taste: Like fruit and flowers and sugar. This is one to pour onto pancakes; very liquid-sweet, and when I say fruit I mean something between green grapes and yellowgages without the sour skin. Juicy sweet is this.

When first I came to the land of Nod
I sought only the blackest locust flowers;
I did not seek a god.

But the fragrance rising from the sod!
I did not expect such honeyed hours
when first I came to the land of Nod!

I expected blossoms, fruit to prod
with careful fingers, pleasant showers;
I did not seek a god.

The grapes that glistened against the broad
green earth, I ate by tree-topped towers.
When first I came to the land of Nod

I came to study, to slowly plod
my way—but now I gorge, devour.
I did not seek a god

to make me mumble like a clod
as sweet within my mouth went sour.
When first I came to the land of Nod
I did not seek a god.

DAY 14 ~ RASPBERRY HONEY

Colour: The dark gold of apple juice, or strong green tea.

Smell: Brown honey smells, hay and a bit of molasses.

Taste: Texture-wise: tending towards crystallising, but not there yet. Almost gelatinous on the wand, but there are bits dreaming of being sugar clumps when I put it against my tongue. It's sweet—dries your mouth out. It makes me think of flower petals, of attar, without tasting of any particular kind that I can distinguish.

Night, come shut my wild, wild eyes,
come pillow my head with thistledown
come gentle me to sleep.

I walked so far for you today,
through markets maddened as the dawn
that rose thrashing from its flush-stained sheets
to rip you from the sky.

I found honey to dress your dawn-dealt wounds
jams to sweet your weeping tongue
juniper to numb the pain
and ink to fill you up.

Take these four kisses on your brow
take this velvet winding sheet,
take these words I've written you
and swallow them with tea.

I've worked so hard for you today,
and I am weary, emptied all—

and all I want is a little bed
with a curved moon swinging
and another in the room, singing.

Day 15 ~ Hungarian Forest Honey

Colour: A cloudy orange-yellow, which, in the first light I held it to, made me think of extra virgin olive oil. In the current light, more of an apple cider.

Smell: Hay, brown sugar, molasses. I held this vial in hot water for about a minute because it was too crystallised to draw enough out on the wand; prior to heating I thought it smelled a bit resinous, but I can't find a trace of that now.

Taste: Brown sugar—cookies! No aftertaste—elusive, like it makes an appearance on request, then vanishes when you aren't paying attention. Also a taste of dark raisins.

※

I lost a ring to the forest, once.

It was a silver ring, plain as rain, and I loved it. It had been a Christmas gift from a dear friend of our family, and I always wore it on the middle finger of my right hand. I was a small girl then, dazzled by the snow on the dark green leaves, dazzled by the cold and the pink in my sister's cheeks. It was rare for us to see it, living in the south as we did, by the sea. But winter in the mountains, where the cedars crowded the slopes like a curious audience, was something else altogether.

The day was sunny. The snow sparkled with it. It was new fallen and a little damp, just enough to pack into snowballs. We played, my sister and I, we rolled about in it, wet our hair, our necks, laughed as we shivered. We rolled a snowman together, and I went into the forest to find branches for his arms.

It was darker there; I scrabbled about the pine and cedar roots, dug into the snow with bare fingers for a prize. To my delight, I found pine branches with a fringe of green needles at the tip that would serve for fingers. I ran back to my sister, laughing that our snowman would be a gardener, would make things grow out of winter, and perhaps, when he melted, he would season the spring with his bones.

She asked, "Where is your ring?"

I looked at my hands, and the laughter caught in my throat like thorns. It was gone. My pink-tipped fingers were bare.

I looked around the snowman, I retraced my steps to the forest. I kicked the snow, trying not to cry, failing. I looked, and looked, and couldn't find it.

My mother was too kind to show me disappointment. She gave me anise tea sweetened with honey, since my throat was sore with crying. She told me to hope for spring, said that we'd return then, and perhaps if I hoped very hard I would find it after the snow had melted—but not to expect that I would. Hope for the best and expect the worst, she said, and tucked me in to bed.

I hoped. I hoped as hard as I had for anything. I felt it was a nightmare, this loss, and if I shut my eyes against it tightly enough it would fade like a dream in the dawn. I would pass hours in which I thought nothing of it during the day, but every night I would remember the lost ring, think of it alone in a forest, rusting and cold, and I would cry a little, and hope a lot.

The winter passed as winters do, and on a bright day in March we returned to the mountains, to the forest. I asked my sister to come with me, to hold my hand as I looked; I was almost afraid of how unhappy I would be, but I told myself to expect nothing, to expect pine needles and earth and nothing else, no metal glinting between rock and root.

We stepped into the forest together. We looked around. Everything looked so different without the snow, looked so much more attentive. We whispered together, because it seemed rude to raise our voices when so many trees were doubtless holding conversations too slow and quiet for us to hear.

Then we saw it.

It seemed an odd bush, at first, but it was in fact a tiny tree. Its trunk was pale as birch, paler, snow-pale and bright, with something very like veins flushing silver beneath the bark.

Rings grew from it like apples. Pale rings, dark rings, green rings and brown. Some of wood, some of bone, some of clay—and one, just one, of silver.

My sister said it was the snowman who'd done it, said that she saw two pine branches nearby that looked very familiar. I don't know, myself. All I know is that I lost a ring to the forest, once, and it was kind enough to give it back.

Day 16 ~ Blueberry Honey

Colour: The exact shade and clarity of apple juice from concentrate.

Smell: Juicy-sweet, with such a faint blueberry scent I could almost be sure I was imagining it. But I'm more sure it's there.

Taste: Blue and cold. Water on a bright day, so blue as to challenge those who would call the water colourless, a sky-mirror. It's a deep blue, and it's a liquid honey, the flexible kind that spindles itself into shapes when stretched. Active, passionate, deep.

I knew you, once.

I knew your hair, the black heat of it. I knew the turn of your instep.
I knew the shadow at your breast on the paper of your skin,
and it drew me in like ink.

I knew the twist of your lips into a secret fit to kiss,
the belly-warm laugh that drew the moth in me too near.
I knew I did not know enough, and you knew how to be kind;
dimmed to push me back, keep my dusty wings unsinged.

But how beautiful you were, how I hovered 'round the glow!
Wanting only to touch, to sip the honey of that heat
without feeding it. My own body so small, so frail,
so simple and so brown,
cindered in the glory of your consummation—
it did not seem a trade worth making.

You knew this, once. I sought to live
by your wisdom, but close by, close as I could dare.
Until you said—until your honey mouth
sang flame and hematite to me—
come near, my little love, come nearer now to me,
I flicker and I dim, and I gutter now and then,
I hunger and I long, and you flutter prettily,
and your dust has known such air, I so long to breathe it in.
Come nearer, my winged girl, come nearer now to me.

I knew you once. I thought I did,
and thought I knew myself as well.
My little body, tiny wings,
though small, still yet my very own.
But I cannot see, cannot be sure,
if in this fragile frame of mine,
if in this dust, I have the strength
to come to know you twice.

Dᴀʏ 17 ~ Uɢᴀɴᴅᴀɴ Hᴏɴᴇʏ

Colour: Cloudy mulled cider—mulled because the crystallised chunks in it make me think of orange peel.

Smell: Carob molasses and hay.

Taste: A savoury flavour: black olives and smoked cheese. It's so unusual, so earthy.

⊰❦⊱

There is a land called Loved-by-the-Sun that is known for its honey. Its flavour is such that the great and small alike seek it out, princes for rarity, peasants for nourishment. It is said that a family can live off an ounce of this fabled honey for a month, and need nothing but water to supplement their meals; it is said that even the rich, smoky scent of it imparts vigour to the mind and limbs, and folk marvel at what flower could produce the nectar necessary to its magic.

They marvel awry. It is all in the tenacity of the bees.

The bees of Loved-by-the-Sun are not content with the search and the find and the dance so common to their tribe. Instead, before they begin the matter of seeking out flowers, they seek out dry brush and twigs. Six or seven will set upon a bit of wood or grass, and though their wings droop and weep with the heft of it, they bring it back to the hive.

Then there is a dance.

One bee, chosen for her beauty, her skill, her strength, will carefully build a dry wall around herself. She will position its materials delicately, in the pattern most appropriate to combustion. Trapped within, she begins to work her wings, rubs her fragile feet against the wood and the hay, and does not stop until she has kindled a flame and fed her body to it.

It is a magnificent spectacle to behold—but more magnificent still is the dance of the other bees. For one by one, they twirl themselves in the smoke of her sacrifice; one by one, they singe their feet on her pyre; one by one, they seek out the noblest flowers and stamp cinders into stamens and pistils, mix their sister's ash with their food. In this way they bless each flower they visit, and one could say with great certainty that all the blossoms of field and forest lean out towards the flight of Loved-by-the-Sun's bees, who scent the air in their wake with solemnity and grace.

Day 18 ~ Manuka Honey

Colour: Mulled cider—but more specifically the dark froth that gathers at the top. This one is also cloudy, with darker splotches in some parts.

Smell: Medicinal. Eucalyptus? A bit like lemon candy, too.

Taste: It tastes like medicine, like cough syrup. I asked my sister to try it for a second opinion, because it tasted like something very specific from our childhood, but while she said medicine, she couldn't narrow it down any further. Cough syrup it remains—or what cough syrup should have tasted like, had it actually been taken with honey.

Thin, scraping. That's how the voices were. Grey and harsh and angry, but thin, above all, thin and scratching as smoke in the throat. I could hear them as through a mist, while lying in my bed, could hear them arguing together.

I was four years old, and didn't know what to do. I thought it must be my parents, and so I got out of bed, hurried past the closet with the skeleton in it, away from dreams of giant spider creatures and vicious monsters with shaggy black fur and bulbous red noses, out of my room and around the corner to my parents.

They were in their beds, asleep.

I could still hear the voices coming from upstairs; I knew that no one else could be up there. But it wasn't the thought that they were in my house that was frightening. It was that they sounded so angry, and that they seemed to be arguing about me.

I curled up on the bottom stairs and cried. It was so hard to know what to do. I had none of the dream-clarity, then, none of the terror that pushes you to run while your legs churn molasses and the monsters gain, none of the exhilaration that forces flight from a cliff-top as the only alternative to pursuit. All I knew was that their voices were wrong, and I wanted them to stop.

So I climbed the stairs. My eyes stung and my cheeks were wet when I saw the ravens.

There were three of them. They perched on our kitchen table, huge as raccoons, and spoke in human voices. As I stood staring at them, they paused, then cocked their heads to look at me in that way that birds do, slantwise.

"Please stop fighting," I whispered. "I want to sleep."

They looked at each other. They looked back at me. One of them hopped a little closer, still on the table. I could see the marks its talons made in the marble-painted wood.

"What you mean," he said—he had a man's voice, anyway— "is that you want to dream."

"Yes," said another, approaching his fellow, "you want the good dreams, the flying dreams."

"Stop," said the third, and here was the woman's voice, weary and sharp as needles. "Leave her alone. She's not ripe."

I didn't know what to say. It didn't seem necessary to speak, not yet. They weren't arguing anymore, anyway, so I kept looking at them. Glossy, the light glinting white and blue from their feathers, their hematite beaks. They were beautiful—much lovelier than seagulls, I remember thinking.

"Do you like honey?" asked the first crow.

"I don't know," I said, truthfully. I hadn't tried any yet. I thought the woman-crow made a sound like sighing.

"Here," said the second crow, and I don't know where he'd dipped his beak, I don't know what pot was open where, but he had something shiny sticking to it, like glue or syrup. "Try this. You may find you like it very much."

I inched closer. I wanted to. I thought I shouldn't, that these were strangers, that my parents and teachers and countless television commercials had told me not to accept things from strangers, especially not food—but this strangeness was comfortable, somehow, almost comforting, now that there was no fighting. I leaned forward to lick the crow's beak—and caught a whiff of what was on it.

It smelled like medicine. I wrinkled my nose, stepped back, and shook my head.

"No thank you," I said, firmly. "I only take medicine from my mommy."

If crows could look disappointed, this one and his friend certainly did. The woman-crow looked... Different. Relieved, maybe. They didn't say another word to me; I looked away for a moment, and when I looked again, they were gone.

I know it's strange I should tell this to you. I know it sounds like madness. But I feel I need to, because this honey you've offered, this sweetness you've mixed into my tea—it smells just like that medicine. And the more I look at you, the more I listen to your kind grey voice, the blacker I find your hair, the darker your eyes, and the sharper your long grey fingers.

DAY 19 ~ HONEYDEW HONEY

Colour: Apple juice. I want to organise these into series; apple juice, apple cider, white wine, various other booze.

Smell: That body smell, ringed with green-fleshed melon that gives the scent a supple thickness.

Taste: Melon, pie, and pistachio.

Morning tastes of honeydew and the fading of candles. It tastes of fingers on guitar strings, of a voice the colour of dimmed lights singing. It tastes of green honey and spring. So spoke the cloudy-haired woman who stood by country roads, near rivers, between beech trees and birch. Her fingers wore no rings, her wrists no bracelets, her feet no shoes.

No one believed her, of course. Who could properly taste the morning?

The morning, she would say, *always tastes of spring, no matter what the season. The winter sun tastes of wet bark and sticky buds when it first rises; at noon it tastes of spun sugar, at evening it tastes of bay leaves and soup. The fall morning tastes of wet grass remembering the sun, the summer morning tastes of lilacs and the waking of bees. And spring mornings taste of honeydew honey, and spring.*

Still no one believed her. *Show us,* they said. *Feed us.*

So she did. She robbed the sky of honey, stole eggs from the sun, ground the dawn to flour. She sifted it through a net of spring branches, salted it with morning-bright sea. She baked bread of the morning, made it into pie-crusts and scones, broke Venus into sultanas and pistachios. She offered them up to passersby, saying only *taste, taste, and tell me what you hear. Robin song sweet enough to sip? Larks and sparrows chittering crumbs and seeds to the ground? Tell me what you see, what you smell. Only taste.*

They tasted. They chewed the dawn with open mouths, swallowed in great lumps.

They shrugged.

It tastes like bread, they said. *Nothing really tastes like spring. Spring doesn't taste like anything.*

She can be found along country roads, near rivers, by beech trees and birch, wherever there are hives. She is most often alone, and birds will not touch the bread she scatters to them; it tastes too much of salt.

Day 20 ～ Blackberry Honey (2)

Colour: Thick, cloudy, creamy orange yellow.

Smell: Sugared brambles and thorns.

Taste: Gentle, quiet; somewhat crystallised. It does not taste of blackberries so far as I can tell; oh, maybe a little, there, but it's more honey than anything else.

It's gone, now.
It's gone, it's passed,
the need, the flush,
dead now, and gone.
The honey on the brambles is melted all to rain,
the sugar on the thorn is licked clean away
and not even a spot of blood to tell its passing. Gone,
and where the tongue to sing of sweetness? Where
the candied throat to chime music to the air,
the lips that want kissing? Gone, I say,
folded thickly into night and swallowed away.

Ophelia went to the river with flowers in her hair,
the river came to Ophelia with fern in his.
She loved the river, drank him down;
he loved Ophelia, took her tears.
They swallowed each other like spoonfuls of salt
and they sang and sang, until, together,
they came to know the sea.

Day 21 ~ Bamboo Honey

Colour: Orange amber, complete with cloudiness and bubbles.

Smell: Thick and gummy; raisins; a hint of molasses.

Taste: Lychee. Completely. Strong, beautiful, lychee-thickened-with-honey with a side of light raisins.

∘✲∘

The air is green as lychee-shine when she knocks at your door. It's early, and you've only just stumbled out of bed, only just finished your second yawn of the day when you shuffle towards the door, stifling the third, wondering who it could be.

You squint at her woman's shape, because your glasses are still by the bed. She seems nice enough.

Let me in, she says, and her voice is friendly, *I have quince and pears to bake, I have honey and raisins and home-made crusts, and your kitchen is very fine.*

You let her in, because you can smell fruit in the air around her, and while you can't quite make out her shape, you figure you'll do her a good turn. Great way to start the day, isn't it, with pie?

You shower while she lays out her things, and through the steam you can hear her singing a song about a chimbley sweep and a wicked dame, and you scrub extra hard behind your ears to show your hospitality. You put on a clean pair of jeans and a dark shirt that shows you're trying, thick socks, even a silver ring on the middle finger of your right hand, and step out into the kitchen.

You forget your glasses. This is not unusual. Also, you look better without them.

She stops singing when you appear, and you suspect she's smiling. Everything smells so good, of browning crust and juicy filling, and you think to ask her name. *Would you like some pie?* she asks, and she smiles, you think she smiles, so you say, sure, when it's ready, is it?

Not quite yet, she says, and her voice is like sugar-water, liquid-sweet and clear. You run your fingers through your hair and say you'll be right back.

You go to your room, pick up your glasses. You figure she's seen how hot you are without them, now she'll find how clever you can look with them on. You adjust them on your nose, and step back out into the kitchen, curious to see what the blurred outlines of the singing woman will resolve into, curious about her age, the colour of her eyes.

She's still a blur.

You blink, take the glasses off, wipe the lenses on your shirt—it's a blend, it'll do—put them back on. You can see the edges of the kitchen counter clear as morning, the lines of the fridge, the cupboard handles, but she, at the center of it all, she's indefinite, she's smudged.

Oh, she says, looking up—you suppose she was looking down. *You're staring. How rude.*

You take a step back, but it's too late. There's a buzzing now, you can tell, a buzzing in the air. *I've half a mind not to feed you any pie*, she says, mildly, *but I can hardly eat it all myself.*

You can't move while you look at her, and you can't look away. There's a razor-sharp piece of quince pie laid out on a plate for you, and its clarity's born up by a cloudy space of skin that's coming closer and closer. *Taste it*, she says. *You'll like it. It tastes like you.*

You taste it. It's like nothing you've had before. She says the same thing to you once you've eaten the slice entire, when you've licked the quince jelly and the crumbs from the plate, when her fruit's inside you. *You're like nothing I've had before*, she says, and you're sure, now, that she's smiling.

DAY 22 ~ MALAYSIAN RAINFOREST HONEY

Colour: Opaque, creamy orange-brown—a bit like pale caramel, slightly warm.

Smell: Cold wet flowers tangled in syrup.

Taste: A very watery honey, strange because it's very crystallised, but it's as if the crystals are floating in wetness. It tastes like candy—the hard kind that come in bright colours, individual wrappers. That, and violets— the scent of violets.

She has eyes like penny candy—one violet, one raspberry blue. There's mischief tucked into her crooked smile's corner, peeking out like a napkin from a tatty pocket. She licks her lips like they're covered in sugar, makes you want to do the same. Her hair's a honey-tangle of brown and blonde, and she's all sweetness and light, sweetness and light put on for show. She has a plum-coloured, corduroy newsboy cap bottom-up in front of her, full of spare change.

"Be careful," say your brother, your sister, your sister's friend. "She has a reputation."

Her voice makes you hungry. She tells you stories whenever you walk by—every time a different one. There's a drum in her throat, you think, beats out a rhythm to reel you in.

"Be careful," she says, smiling. "There's a troll lives by that trash can, will trip you every time."

You look down, blushing, walk a little faster—trip, and flush hotter. You turn back, and she's laughing a little, but you don't hold it against her.

"Be careful," she says, grinning, "There's a water-thing 'round that spout that'll suck the air from your flames."

You can't light a cigarette all day to save your life. But you like her, you can't help it, and every day you drop a few quarters her way, shy, flustered, grateful.

"Be careful," she says, one day, and the candy in her eyes is rock-hard, "there are faces in the stone walls, watching, waiting for you to turn your back before pouncing."

You freeze. You can't look at anything but her solemn face, until she stands up, tips the coins out of her cap and into your palm, pats your shoulder seriously.

"You need the change," she says, settling the cap on her honey hair. "Be careful. It's time to go."

She reaches out her hand, and you take it.

Day 23 ~ Tart Cherry Creamed Honey

Colour: The colour of quince syrup: a dark beautiful red amber.

Smell: I wonder what it is about creaming honey that produces that unpleasantness? All the creamed ones have had it so far, an odd body-like odour that I'm coming to realise promises deliciousness. There's a sharpness to this one too, though, a hint of pine resin.

Taste: Cherries steeped in syrup or wine.

There's music around her when she moves towards him, determined, lips numb and cheeks flushed. She's watched him all evening, heard him laugh, memorised the cadence of his speech, waited for it. She's been drinking cherry cordial, pretending to listen to the words addressed to her, smiling when appropriate, nodding her head. But the night is almost over now, and she walks towards him.

His hair is black, his skin is pale. He's like something out of a storybook, she thinks, and she wants him to speak to her, wants to meet his eyes, wants to dazzle him with her cleverness, with her kohl-lined eyes and short skirt and the strength of her want.

I will take you, she will say, *to a place you've never been, because I know, I can tell, that you've never known eyes like mine. I will take you to a corner as dark as it is quiet and I will tell you the story of a pale-skinned boy who dreamt of a girl with eyes like mine, and it will enchant you like a song heard at midnight by a jasmine-petaled pool. You will hear it and you will see me by the story's light, you will want my lips at your ear and my words against your skin, and you will tell me I taste of cherry cordial and I will tell you how you smell of tobacco and molasses and we will leave together, we will leave hand in hand and discover each other one new word at a time.*

She approaches him. He laughs, as he has been laughing all evening, but this time he looks at her as he does it. He looks at her and he laughs, and she meets his eyes as he does, and his laughter breaks her thoughts to pieces. Her lips part without sound, meet again; she cannot move. She closes her eyes, steps back, steps away, turns towards the door, and purse in hand she pushes it open and walks out into the night.

He does not follow; he never saw her. He has never wondered at her name.

Day 24 ~ Apricot Creamed Honey

Colour: Today's booze-related colour is lager, specifically Beck's.

Smell: In keeping with creamed honey form, more belly-button fuzz!

Taste: A juicy sweetness, fresh; the honey's liquidy, and the sweetness has a liquid edge to it as well. It doesn't dry out the mouth at all, and calls up fruit without tasting specifically of apricot.

The bees come when she lets down her hair.

There is a simple brass stick, two-pronged, with which she binds it up until the moment is precisely right. When she leans over a railing to gaze at the sea; when she bites into an apricot and closes her eyes; when the rain ends and the air drips with the scent of wet leaves, she pulls the stick from her hair, releases it, lets it tumble down in chestnut waves. It smells of honey and ginger, and the bees love it.

When they surround her, she breathes in the vibration of their bodies, exhales music, breathes it in again. They crown and armour her, they hide her while she dissolves into a joy too keen for eyes that come in simple pairs, eyes that could not possibly appreciate the peace, the thrill, the trembling, the way those thousand bodies do. They sing her aching silence out, they chime their wings like champagne flutes, they pat her cheeks and lashes with more love than is commonly thought to be possible. *You smell so good, so good*, they cry, *we love the way you smell*. And when the trembling subsides, when their joy ebbs like a wave from the sand, they bestow a final kiss against her hair, her skin, before flying off.

She gives them so much. She gives them all she can. And so it is only natural and proper that they give her something in return.

There are days where the hair-stick falls, days when her curls bounce against her shoulders with a dimmed shine, days when her hair smells less of honey than of salt, of ash, of pitch. There are days when the bees come and find her curled up against a wall, days when the sea clings to her lashes, when no sun nor storm lights up the sky, when she forgets the taste of fruit. On those days the bees know what to do.

They come, they gather around her, they form a black-banded ribbon of gold from their hive to their quarry. Each comes bearing a lick of honey in her mouth, presses it against the girl's in a kiss. They offer her honey made of sun and sea, honey made of apricots, honey made of rain-wet leaves. They offer her honey scented with the ginger of her hair. One kiss at a time, they fill up what she has spilled from herself, never speak of the mess it's made on the rug.

Each one says to her, as she sips from them as best she can, *remember*.

DAY 25 ~ RAW MANUKA HONEY

Colour: Pale cloudy yellow, the colour of late morning light.

Smell: Strongly anti-septic; a cleaning product smell.

Taste: It's thick without being crystallised, heaps out onto the wand, and tastes clean and sugary without the chemical smell interfering. A flavour not dissimilar to anise.

She curls up on the beach at night, limbs tucked in tight as coral, just shy of the tide's reach. She does not let it touch her for fear of a knife's edge on her skin, for fear of a longing so keen it would slice her heart in two. But nestled close, half-burrowed into the sun-warmed sand, she can almost imagine herself in the water.

Give us your hair, they said, *and we will take such care of you. You will never want, save when you touch the sea; you will never hurt, save when you seek the waves. You will never want home, never need anything more than the sun and the sand and your husband's body, and all other love will fade to foam in the dawn.*

There is a ring on her finger. It hurts when she tries to take it off, digs deep grooves into her skin.

Her husband is a Good Man. He dutifully inquires after her day at dinner, dutifully nods his head when she answers, dutifully makes love to her in the wide feather bed they share every second evening.

She used to dance, she remembers that. She used to dance to her own singing. She would lift her arms above her head and jewel-coloured fish would swarm about them like bees, darting between the long strands of her green hair, through the space between her fingers. She never needed kisses, then; her mouth was for eating, for music, nothing else.

You will have a husband who tastes like bread and salt, they said. *What need will you have of fins, of gills, of ocean storms?*

She believes him when he says he loves her. She does not believe herself, anymore.

An overzealous wave reaches the tip of her finger, and she cries out as if cut. No blood wells up, no parting can be seen in her perfect skin. Water is not, after all, sharp.

All she wants is to sleep as she used to. All she wants is to close her eyes and feel warm, to feel the salt flushing her arms, scouring her tail. But the sea-bees have made a hive of the hair she gave them, and she cannot swim without it, cannot have a tail without something to comb.

She presses a kiss into the sand; it cuts where it's moist. Quickly, before she can change her mind, she lifts herself into the sea, shatters the glass surface of it, cries out when its shards carve a path inward, deeper and deeper, soaking her through.

There is a great deal of foam, come morning. It tastes strangely sweet.

Day 26 ~ Blackberry Creamed Honey

Colour: Red as melted garnets, Pinot Noir, blackberry syrup cut with water. This is the reddest honey I've seen yet.

Smell: *Qurban*, the bread served at funerals.

Taste: The honey takes a back seat to the blackberry. It's like a blackberry syrup, like *toot*, mulberry syrup my mother would mix up with water to make us a summer drink. Delicious, sweet and smooth.

He is bitter as ash left cold on the grate,
white as soured milk, wry as bread left to spoil
and very, very sad. He smiles a twist of fennel
every now and then, laughs anise and asphodel,
but buries it beneath a deep, damp soil
that grows nothing but rye.

He carries an amphitheatre in his back pocket,
pulls it out when company calls,
breaks his voice against its walls and makes them echoes, keeps
a cedar forest between them and him, a host of shattered sounds
to splinter the ear.

She comes prepared.

She stops her ears with brown beeswax,
slicks her lips with garnet wine,
blackberry honey, a touch of mint,
hides cardamom beneath her tongue
and knocks against his door.

Out come the echoes, six by eight,
ten by twenty-two, in octagons
and triangles, all sharp, all edged as teeth
to worry her to the stoop, push her out,
hedge himself away.
You're mad, he says, *you're mad as mad*
you're silly and small, and so naive,
you speak too much and laugh too loud,
you tire me.

She walks towards him, tangles them. *Don't worry,*
she says, *I've done this before,*
and takes his milk, his bread, his ash,
his fennel and anise, his rye,
draws them close against her blackberry mouth
and swallows them all down.

The air is still when she's done with him,
turns her back on his ash-grate hair,
leaves him quiet and crunching on cardamom,
licking honey from his lips.

DAY 27 ~ LEATHERWOOD HONEY

Colour: Chardonnay. I look at its pale yellow-gold and imagine the buttery aftertaste. Beautifully, stickily liquid and clear.

Smell: Candy-sweet with a creaminess to it, white flowers and sugared milk.

Taste: High sweetness; on the register of sweetness this would a top note. A sweetness you taste behind your eyes. Petals and light.

To be given honey is a great gift, fraught with special significance. As Victorians chose their nosegays, as they elaborated a language of petal and thorn and stem, so too is there a language of honey, a dialect of nectar and pollen, that must be learned and recited in appropriate situations.

To give clover honey says *I am a fair-weather friend. I am sweet and I am light, and I see the same in you. Let us mix when it is convenient, but never too deeply, for our flavours blend well only when they are similar. Let us be pleasant together.*

To give Manuka honey says *I care for you more than I care for your caring of me. I care for you so much that I will hurt you to see you well, that I will put foulness into your mouth because I know it to be medicine, that I will take your scowls and hatreds and fold them against my heart like a locket full of hair because I will know you to be well.*

One gives raspberry honey for loving friendship between women; buckwheat honey to fathers on Father's Day; red gum honey to a best friend with whom one has quarrelled, seeking solace. One gives rose honey to girls with brown eyes, black locust honey to boys with green, in token of gentle, unassuming love.

Leatherwood honey is rarely given, for it signifies commitment of a deeper sort.

I want you, it says, *because your skin lacks my mark on it. I want to push you against a wall and twist your arm behind your back and breathe against your neck to show you my want, to show you how much I value you. I will love you hard and strong because I suffer in loving you, and will make you suffer with me. I will lay honey on a collar and tighten it around your neck the better to lick the excess from its edges, where the red welts show. I will have you for my own, and you will have no choice but to like it.*

To accept leatherwood honey seals an important compact. It is not for the sweet-toothed maiden who has run out of thistle, not for the indifferent young man to whom all sweetness is equal, to whom sour and bitter are much the same thing. One must take it with a gaze full of the giver, and upon receiving a jar of the precious stuff, bow one's head down low.

Day 28 ~ French Chestnut Honey

Colour: Sunshine in Ottawa, and a little paler still.

Smell: More than a flower, something else, something earthy and nutty and malty at once. Hints of green and smoke, substance.

Taste: A burnt wood taste, hints of anise; this is a honey that tastes very brown and black, dark with slants of light in it.

Once upon a time, there was a girl who forgot how to kiss.

It began with touching, as so many things do. She lived in a beautiful place, and as she walked by stone, by leaves, by flowers, a longing rose in her that needed to spill out through her fingertips to reach the petals, the thorns, the grass that prompted it. Where she could not reach the beauty she saw—the clouds, the stars, the moon all being so far away—she touched her lips, instead, and blew them a quiet kiss. They never kissed back, but why should they? She was not an eighth so lovely as they.

But there lay the difficulty. Boys are not so lovely as storms, girls not so lovely as cresting waves, and she, well, why should she be even as lovely as boys or girls? Let the earth take her kisses without cracking, let the water touch her lips without hissing, and she would be content. They did, of course; what was a girl to them? She pressed kiss after kiss to bark and current, blew kiss after kiss to sunlight and shadows, and soon forgot the shape of lips against her own, the taste of honey and salt mixing. She shied away from the gazes of boys and girls, bound her hair in brambles, braceleted her arms in vines, filled her mouth with chestnut honey to say *away, keep away; I have forgotten how to kiss, how to be kissed, and do not want to remember.*

It was the honey that drew the bees.

How they laughed at her astonishment when they nuzzled

her lips! How they danced about her bramble-thick hair, her green-ringed arms! How she all but melted as they kissed and kissed and kissed her, took her kisses to flowers in fields and forests, buried her breath between stamen and pistil! How they dusted her mouth with pollen when they returned!

She kissed their buzzing wings, their stamping feet, their beautiful black-banded bodies. She let them into her mouth, let them scour her tongue of chestnut honey, wept to feel its curious loss, the ache of a wood-burnt aftertaste filling her mouth like incense.

Why are you so sad, girl, you who love us so much? asked the bees, as she wept.

I am sad because I love you, because I love you so much, and because I am not a bee to buzz with you lightly. I am not a flower, not a tree, not a rain-hewn stone. I am not a storm or a cresting wave, not a thorn or a vine. I am not the sun stinging the water, not the moon on the snow. I am not a star in the dark. I am not the dew-wet wind, not the cloud-stained dawn. I am only a girl, a small, plain girl, a girl who must smear her lips in honey to be found sweet.

Oh, said the bees, *oh, oh, oh. But your kisses reach so far, girl, your kisses touch the sky!*

That may be, said the girl, *but they are not enough to please the sky, and so cannot please me.*

Oh! laughed the bees, *oh, oh, oh! You are so silly, you are so sweet! Sweet silly thing, the sky is not a girl!*

The girl said nothing with wide, wild eyes. They laughed with their wings, their feet, their black-banded beauty.

A flower is not a girl, and a tree is not a girl. A stone is not a girl, nor a storm, nor a wave; a thorn is not a girl, nor a vine, nor a star. The sun-stung water is not shaped like a girl, the cloud-stained dawn cannot bind its hair in brambles. But they kiss and kiss and kiss you all the same; can't you feel them? You are a girl, and that is beautiful.

They kissed her one by two by six by twelve, they sipped her tears away. They stamped the brambles from her hair, they slipped the vines from her wrists, they ate the ache from her chestnut mouth. And soon, soon, she learned to see storms in boys' eyes, cresting waves in girls' hair, and tasted honey on every tongue.

Acknowledgments

I have so many people to thank. First, thanks to Danielle, for the generosity and creativity that sparked everything off, and for being the kind of person who inspires me to aspire; next to Catherynne Valente, for accepting a gift of honey from me one February in Ottawa, becoming my dear friend, and introducing me to hers.

Deep, heartfelt thanks are due to Caitlyn Paxson and Mike Allen for their comments and suggestions, but most especially to Claire Cooney, who sank her knuckles into this manuscript and kneaded it as no one else did, who showed me line by line how it could be tightened and sharpened and shaped. Thanks, too, to my sister Dounya, for tasting Manuka honey with me, and to James Williams, for his willingness to keep the strange girl in the wine bar company while she sucked sweetness from unstoppered vials in public.

Thanks to everyone on my Livejournal friendslist who read along as I was writing this day by day of a February; to Nicole Kornher-Stace, who was the first to suggest that these small things should be collected; to Jessica Wick, for the unwitting loan of her Ogress and Dream-Thief; to Deborah Brannon, for putting in time and energy to promote it; and to my parents, for their encouragement, kind words, lullabies, and for reading beyond the Peach Creamed Honey.

I will be forever grateful that Erzebet saw something here worth touching with her bone-sculpting hands, and that Oliver Hunter has lent his unbearable skill to this project. I have always longed to see my words made into art, and am more humbled than I can say that such brilliant artists have engaged with it.

And thanks to you, of course, for reading to the very end.

AMAL EL~MOHTAR

AMAL EL-MOHTAR is a first-generation Lebanese-Canadian, currently pursuing a PhD in English literature at the Cornwall campus of the University of Exeter. Her short fiction and poetry have appeared in a range of publications both online and in print, including *Weird Tales, Strange Horizons, Shimmer, Cabinet des Fées, Sybil's Garage, Mythic Delirium*, and *Ideomancer*; her short fiction has also been broadcast on *Podcastle*. She won the 2009 Rhysling Award with her poem "Song for an Ancient City," and co-edits *Goblin Fruit*, an online quarterly dedicated to fantastical poetry, with Jessica P. Wick.

CPSIA information can be obtained
at www.ICGtesting.com
Printed in the USA
BVHW020808280821
615436BV00001B/12